D0041343

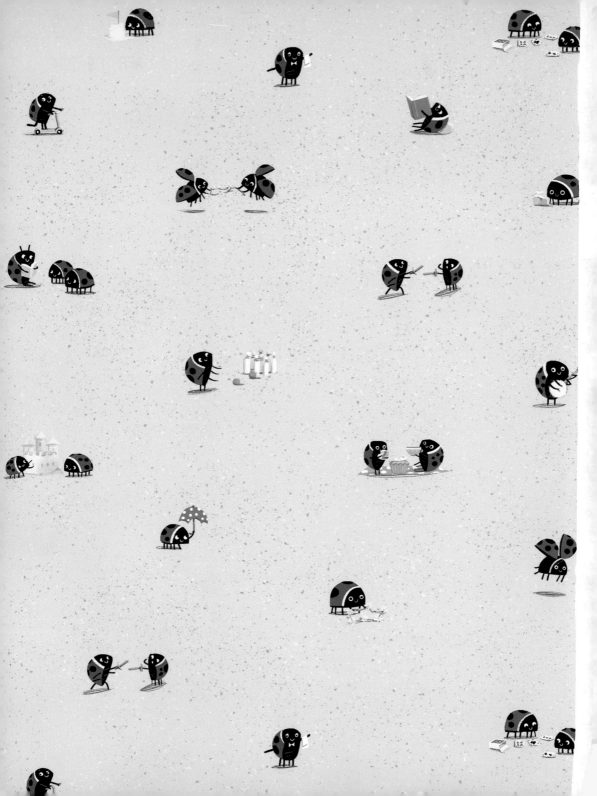

Dedicated to Jody Lewen,
who inspires others during
their long time-outs
-P.L.

To Mama & Papa.
With all my love
-K.E.

Dial Books for Young Readers
Published by the Penguin Group
Penguin Group (USA) LLC
375 Hudson Street
New York, New York 10014

USA / Canada / UK / Ireland / Australia / New Zealand / India / South Africa / China
penguin.com
A Penguin Random House Company

Library of Congress Cataloging-in-Publication Data
Lakin, Patricia, date.
Bruno & Lulu's playground adventures / by Patricia Lakin ; illustrated by
Kirstie Edmunds.   pages cm
Summary: Best friends Bruno the squirrel and Lulu the chipmunk have
adventures, both real and imaginary, on the playground.
ISBN 978-0-8037-3553-8 (hardcover)
[1. Play—Fiction. 2. Imagination—Fiction. 3. Best friends—Fiction. 4. Friendship—Fiction.
5. Squirrels—Fiction. 6. Chipmunks—Fiction.]
I. Edmunds, Kirstie, illustrator. II. Title. III. Title: Bruno and Lulu's playground adventures.
PZ7.L1586Br 2014   [E]—dc23   2012043897

Manufactured in China on acid-free paper
1 3 5 7 9 10 8 6 4 2

Designed by Mina Chung · Text set in Bleeker
This art was created digitally.

Bruno & Lulu's
Playground Adventures

by Patricia Lakin

illustrated by Kirstie Edmunds

 Dial Books for Young Readers
an imprint of Penguin Group (USA) LLC

Table of Contents

Say that you love your scooter, going too fast, swinging too high, playing in our playground, and . . .

And playing with you, my best friend, Lulu.

7

Thank you. Now tell them about me.

Your name is Lulu. You love to pretend, pretend, pretend. Sometimes it gets you in trouble.

8

The Cake

Look, Bruno.
They are eating cake.

I know you, Lulu. You like to pretend. You see a pretend cake. Well, I do not like to pretend.

But you like cake, Bruno. And this cake is real. Look!

Cake! I love cake.

I know! Let's go.

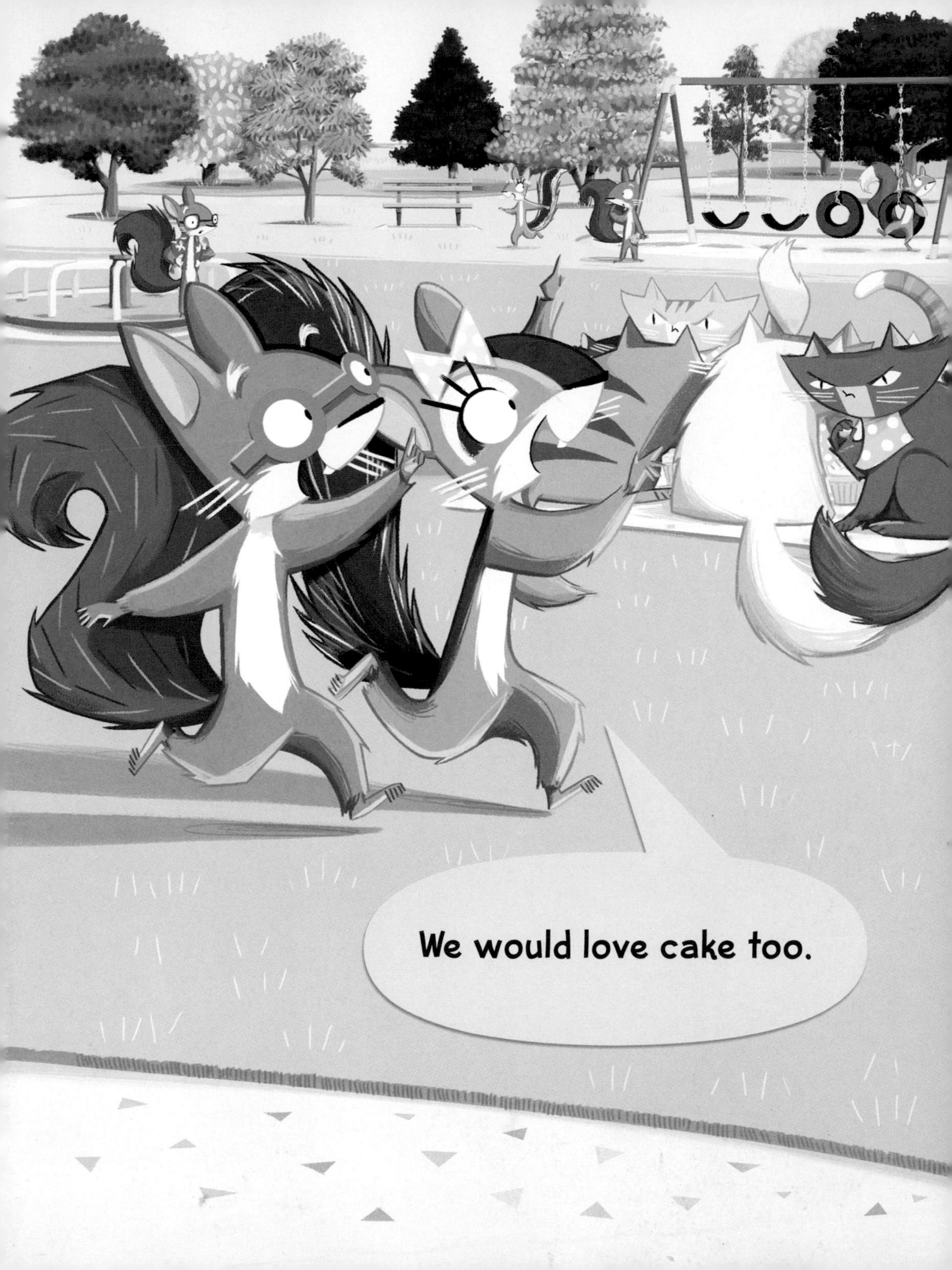
We would love cake too.

21

23

And I am sorry.
You should be.
Yes, I am. I needed that water for our cake.
Aarrgh!

Help me mix.

We cannot eat this.

I know. It is not ready.

. . . even when it is ready.

Why not?

It is not a cake.
It is not a cake I like.

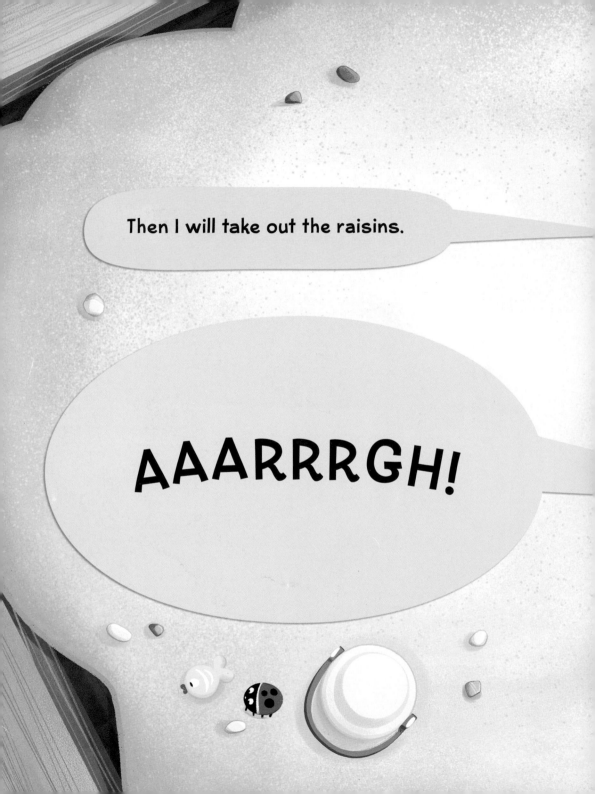

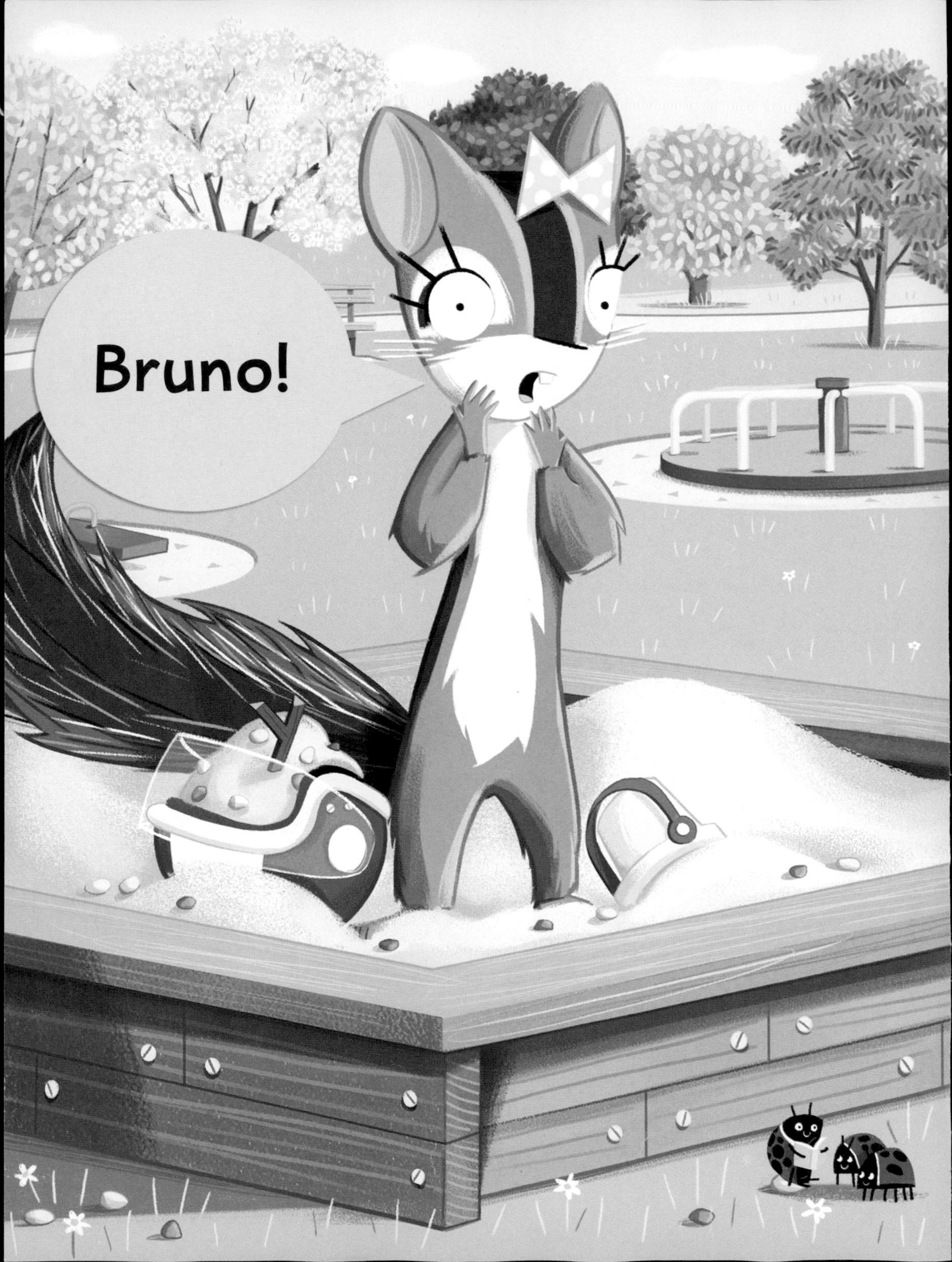
Bruno!

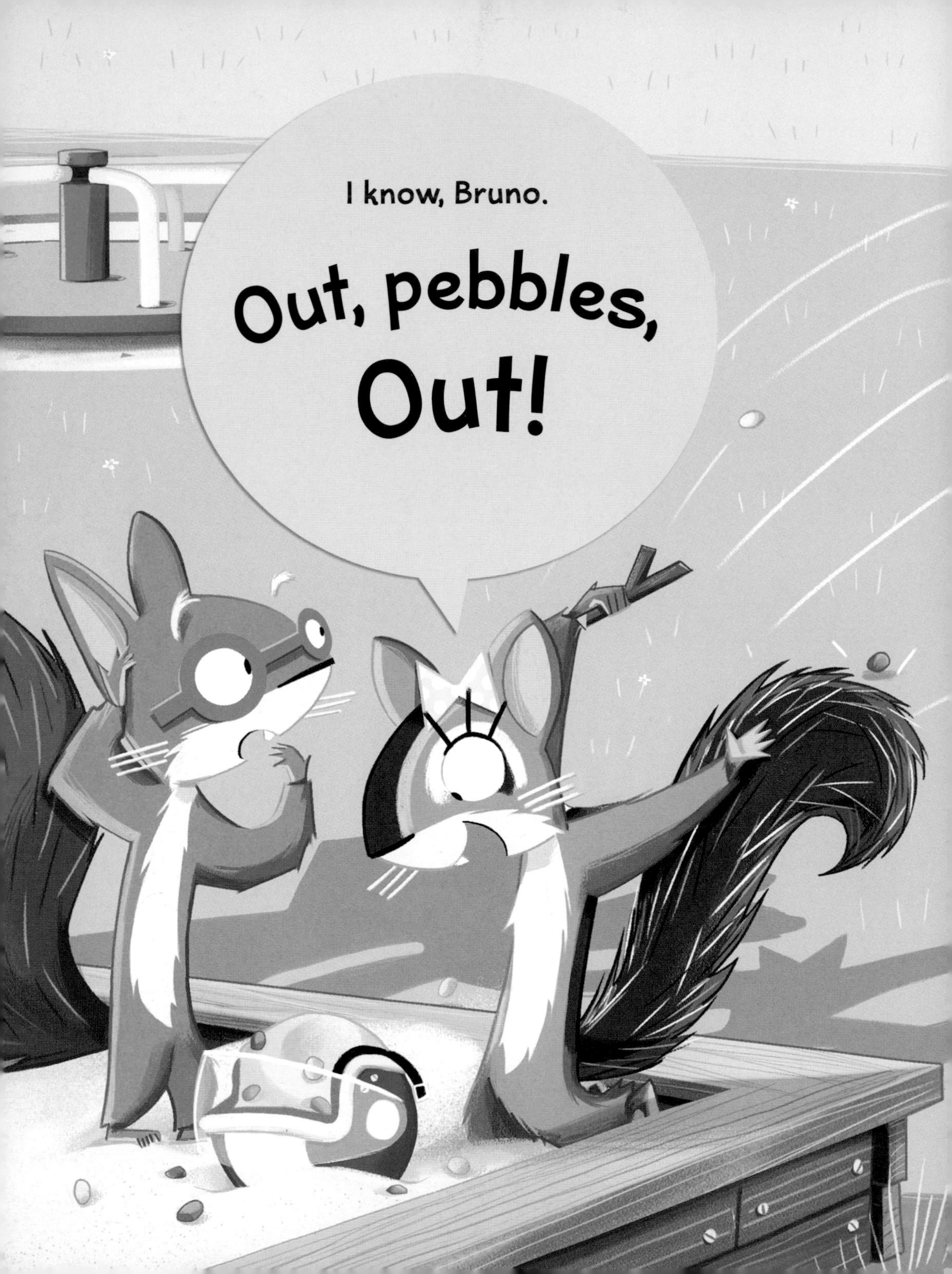
I know, Bruno.
Out, pebbles, Out!

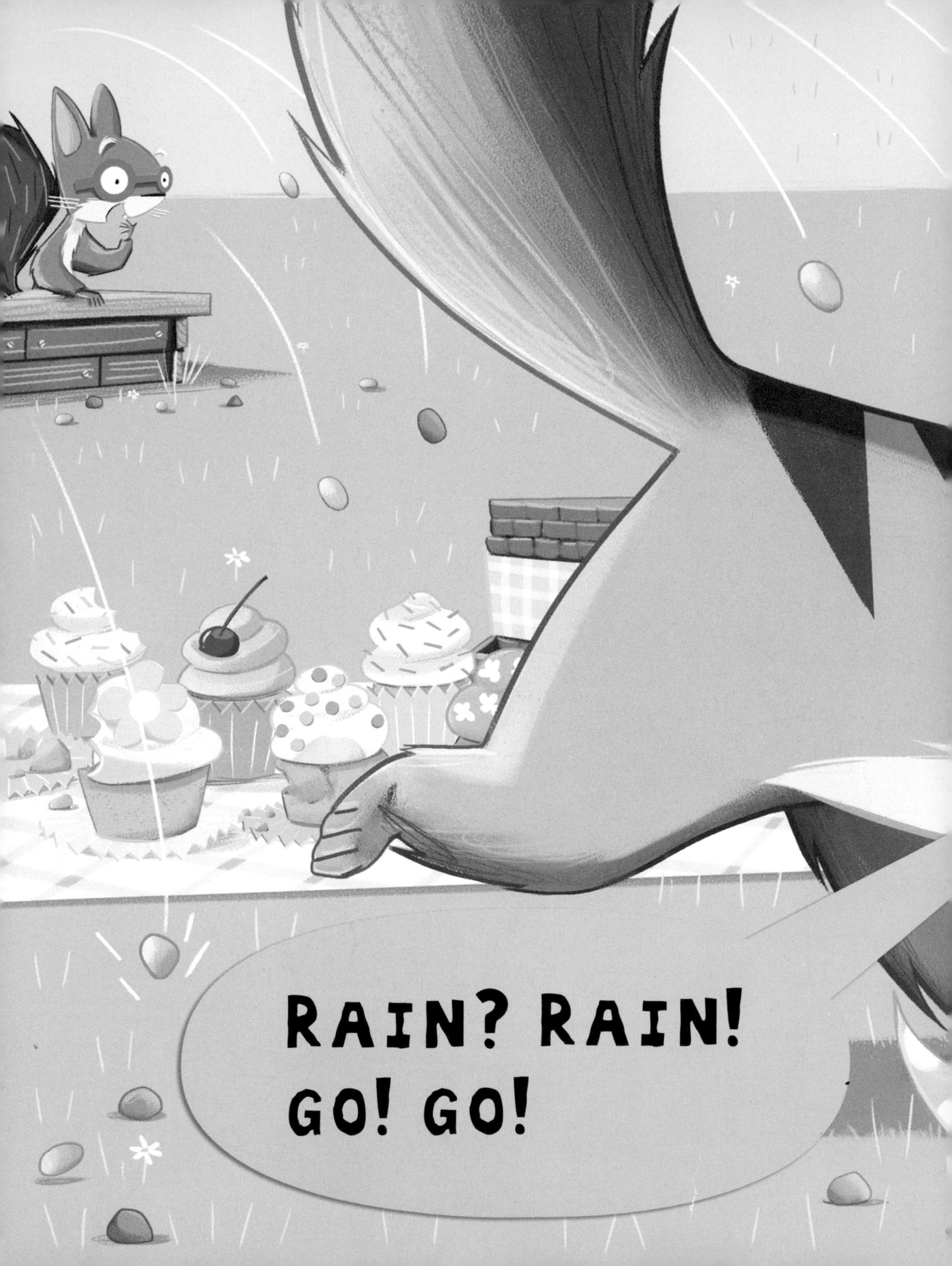
RAIN? RAIN!
GO! GO!

I am busy too, Lulu.

But I am busy throwing.

And I am busy eating.

Eating what?

Eating cake.

You said you did not want their cake.

I know. I was pretending.

How is their cake?

Very good, but . . .

But what?

Time-Out

What did you do?
I forget.
How could you forget?
It is a very loooooong time-out. That's why I forgot.
But I want to play with you.
I want to play with you too.

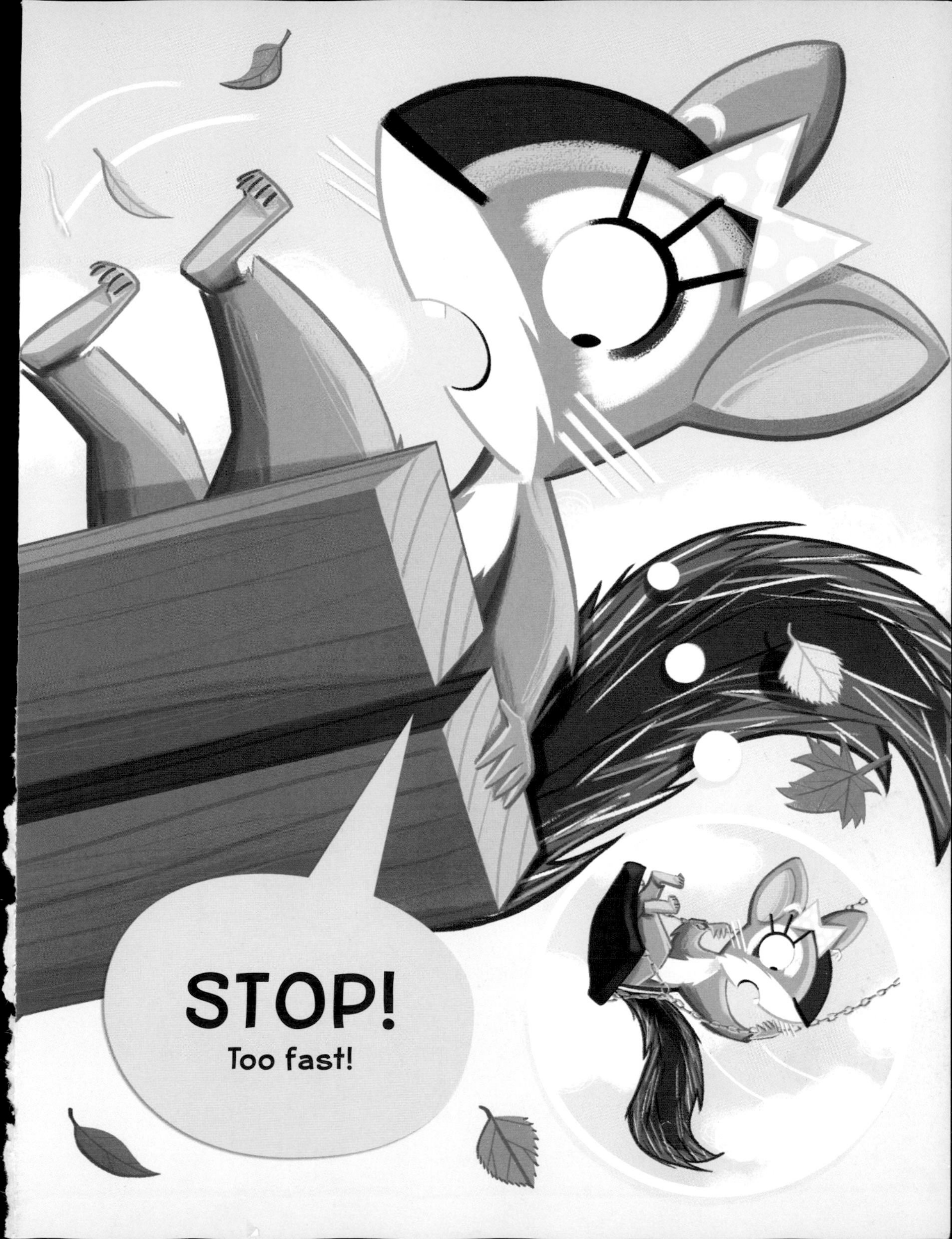
STOP!
Too fast!

Yes. I can fly.
Guess what I am.

You are Flying Lulu.

No. Guess again.

This is too hard.

You do not have to guess.
Why not?
Because I am Bruno!
Errrrkkk!
What else are you?
I am your friend.
I know. But pretend.
What are you?

I am a sad friend.
That is not pretend.
But I know what to do.
And I will be right back.

I am counting to ten.

1 2 3 4
5 6 7
8 9 10

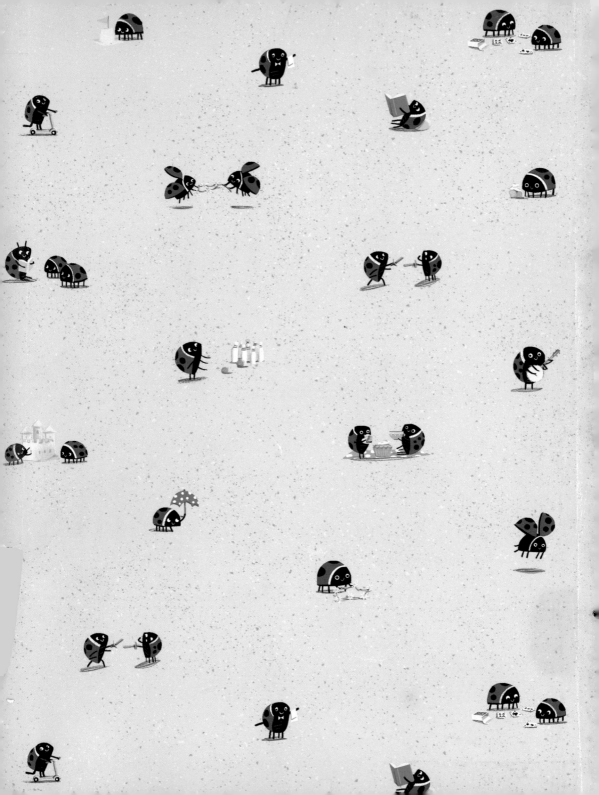